This book was discovered thanks to
the Key Colors Competition China

Copyright © 2021 Clavis Publishing Inc., New York

Originally published as *Regenbooghoedje* in Belgium and the Netherlands by Clavis Uitgeverij, 2020
and as 小彩帽 in China by Yunnan Aurora Publishing House Co., Ltd.
© 2019 Beijing Yutian Hanfeng Books Co., Ltd. for Simplified Chinese and Traditional Chinese
English translation from the Dutch by Clavis Publishing Inc., New York

Visit us on the Web at www.clavis-publishing.com.

Rainbow Hat written and illustrated by Hong Hai

ISBN 978-1-60537-617-2

This book was printed in March 2021 at Nikara, M. R. Štefánika 858/25, 963 01 Krupina, Slovakia.

First Edition
10 9 8 7 6 5 4 3 2 1

Clavis Publishing supports the First Amendment and celebrates the right to read.

Hong Hai

RAINBOW

Hat

Clavis

NEW YORK

Whoosh! Bear's hat is blown away.
Where does the hat go?

To Turtle.
Turtle **walks** calmly to the pond.

Splash! Turtle dives into the water.
Where does the hat go now?

To Frog.
Frog **jumps** out of the water.

Quack! The hat is too big for Frog.
Who's coming?

It's Duck.
Duck **floats** on the water.

Quack! Duck loses the hat in the water.
Where does the hat go now?

To Fish.
Fish **swims** in the water.

Plop! Fish turns around quickly.
Who has the hat now?

It's Bird.
Bird **flies** through the air.

Whoosh! Bird lets go of the hat.
Where does it fly to now?

To **Bear!**
What luck.
The hat still fits perfectly.